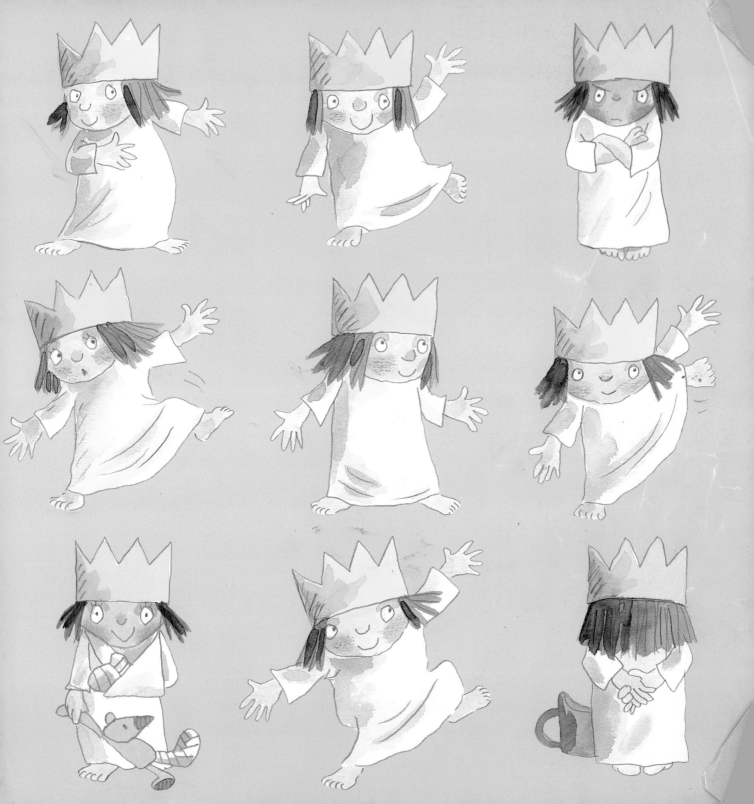

First published in hardback in Great Britain by Andersen Press Ltd in 2001
First published in paperback by Collins Picture Books in 2002

ISBN-13: 978-0-00-778254-3
ISBN-10: 0-00-778254-3

Collins Picture Books is an imprint of the Children's Division, part of HarperCollins Publishers Ltd.

Text and illustrations copyright © Tony Ross 2001, 2002

Visit our website at: www.harpercollinschildrensbooks.co.uk

Printed and bound in Hong Kong

I Want My Dummy

Tony Ross

HarperCollins *Children's Books*

"I want my dummy!"

"You're not still using a dummy?" said the Admiral.
"It's nice!" said the Little Princess.

"This tastes much better than a dummy," said the Cook.
"No, it doesn't!" said the Little Princess.

"Where's my dummy gone?"

"...I want my dummy!"

"How did it get up the chimney?"

"I'll never lose it again!"

"Where's my dummy? I want my dummy!"

"What's it doing under the dog?" said the Little Princess.

"I'll NEVER lose my dummy again!" she said.

"NEVER, never, never, never..."

"Burglars have taken my dummy! I want my dummy!"

"How did it get into the dustbin?"

"It tastes better after a wash!" said the Little Princess.

"It's gone again! I WANT MY DUMMY!"

"How did it get into the pond?"

"I'll never let it go again!" said the Little Princess.
"It's safe on this ribbon."

"Aren't you too grown-up for a dummy?"
said the Prime Minister.
"No!" said the Little Princess.

"Soldiers don't have dummies!" said the General.
"Ladies don't have dummies, either," said the Maid.

"Well I do, SO THERE!" said the Little Princess.

"That dummy looks stupid!" said her cousin.

"It does!" said the Little Princess.
"But it's not mine…"

"...it's Ted's!"